NORMAN THE DOORMAN

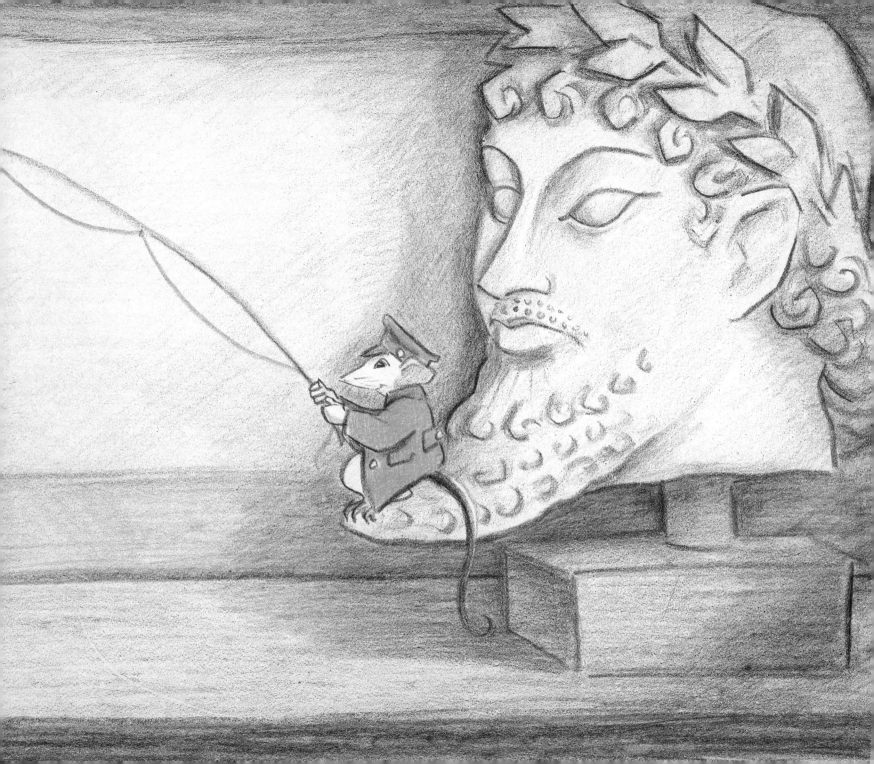

NORMAN THE DOORMAN

BY DON
FREEMAN

To

Doyle and David

Hilary and Tony

Wiggy and Tuni

Stevie and Sarah

Bernard and Curtis, and

with two pieces of cheese

for my nieces, Donna and Patti

NORMAN THE DOORMAN

In front of a small, well-hidden hole around in back of the Majestic Museum of Art there once stood a mouse named Norman.

Norman was a doorman, and he greeted all the art-
loving creatures who came to see the treasures which
were kept in the basement of the museum.

"Come right in!" Norman would say to his cousins
the Petrinis. "We're quite safe. I've sprung all the
traps."

SAD CLOWN
BY CECIL C. BE

Norman would explain every painting in detail
and handle each masterpiece with as much care and
respect as if he had painted it himself!

He would also take great pride in pointing out the artistic features of certain pieces of Greek sculpture which rested in the dark corners of the storage room.

Norman's only worry was keeping out of sight of
the sharp-eyed upstairs guard, who often came to the
basement to set traps for mice!

His bright flashlight frightened the visitors, and they dashed out the secret hole into the night like streaks of pink and white lightning.

As for Norman, he always managed to escape and
hide inside an old armored knight's helmet. Up there
he felt perfectly safe.

Actually the helmet was Norman's home, which he had made into a very comfortable and workable studio. Just see what a splendid skylight the visor made!

Like most everybody, Norman had a hobby. Each
night after work he tried to create something pleas-
ing or beautiful—perhaps a painting of Swiss cheese
and crackers, or a statue.

One bitter cold day Norman decided to stay in his studio and make something out of wire. For some time he had been collecting mousetraps and odd scraps of picture-hanging wire, with the intention of putting them to artistic use.

The mousetraps weren't any good any more, since Norman had cleverly taken out the pieces of cheese and then snapped the traps shut without having harmed even so much as a whisker on his nose.

All through the day and far into the night Norman twisted and bent wires into many strange and mysterious shapes—until, at last, he created something

he was really proud of! It looked for all the world
like a mouse on a trapeze.

That night when he finally went to sleep he was
a tired but very happy mouse.

Early next morning when Norman went outside to shovel away the snow in front of his doorway he noticed a man reading a sign nearby.

He too read the sign—

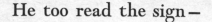

SCULPTURE
CONTEST
OPEN TO ALL ARTISTS,
GREAT AND SMALL!

PRIZES! PRIZES!

WORKS IN
STONE, IRON, BRONZE, WOOD,
OR WIRE WELCOME

LAST DAY TODAY!

Back he flew!

25

"Why can't I show my wire statue?" he said as he slid through the visor-lid opening.

But what would he call it? All pieces must have titles, he well knew.

Suddenly he had an inspiration. Stripping off the printed word "TRAP" from the label, and then ripping off the letters "EESE" from the word "cheese," he pasted them together.

Now he had a fitting title for his wire work! Although Norman was a modest mouse, he practically burst a button off his coat.

Then, as this was the last day for the artists to bring their sculpture pieces in, Norman put a cover over his statue, as he had seen the others do, and away he scooted.

Up the front stairway he climbed, one snowy step at a time.

Once inside the huge museum, he eagerly followed the other sculptors from one room to another. He still had to be extremely careful of the sharp-eyed guard! Contest or not, he didn't want to get caught!

33

After carefully removing the cover from his wire
statue, he left it on the floor with the rest of the con-
testants' work

NINA
BY
XXXXXX

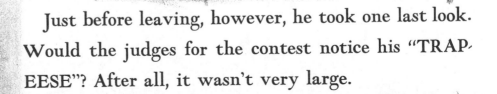

Just before leaving, however, he took one last look. Would the judges for the contest notice his "TRAP-EESE"? After all, it wasn't very large.

Out he went into the snowy afternoon knowing
he had done his best.

Back once more in his helmet studio, Norman went about sewing new brass buttons on his blue coat. You see, he had not forgotten that he was a doorman who had a job to do.

Meanwhile, upstairs in the Sculpture Gallery of the museum, the judges were busy judging. Quietly and seriously they examined each piece, trying to find which ones deserved prizes.

OLD
WREST
BY
H. IN

FIRST
PRIZE
IN
WOOD

THE FISH
THAT GOT
AWAY
BY
L. COOK

Gradually they found themselves huddled around
a certain statue.

39

"Now *this* is an amazing creation!" exclaimed one of the judges.

"There's no name," said another. "And isn't it a shame it's so tiny!"

"Yes, but remember, the contest is open to great and small," said another judge.

One by one each guard, when asked if he knew who had brought it in, shook his head and said, "No, not I." The Museum director couldn't understand why none of them had caught sight of the artist.

But when the sharp-eyed guard took a closer look he gasped. "Oh, so this is where all my mousetraps have been going! I think I know where to start searching for the tricky trap-snatcher!"

Without waiting another minute, the guard
snapped on his flashlight and hurried downstairs to
the basement.

"What's this — one of my traps stuck in a knight's helmet?"

He lifted up the visor to investigate. There inside he saw pieces of wire and parts of traps and — strangest of all — a neat straw bed which could only belong to a mouse.

"Whoever he is, he must be mighty fond of my cheese," said the guard as he knelt down on the floor and pointed the flashlight at some tracks which led out through the hole in the wall.

During all this time Norman had been tending to his duty as doorman. A party of mice from the country, for whom he had been waiting, was long past due, and he was getting mighty cold and hungry.

But, to his surprise, who should be coming around
the corner but the sharp-eyed guard!

"Oho, so there you are!" said the guard as
Norman fled inside.

But when the guard held a piece of cheese just above the hole and Norman sniffed it, he couldn't help poking his nose out to get a better whiff.

And just as he was about to reach up and snatch the cheese, a hand came down swiftly and caught Norman by his tail!

"Say, are you the rascal who's been taking my mousetraps every day and using them for artistic purposes?" asked the guard sternly.

"It's just a hobby!" sobbed Norman. "Just my hobby!"

Right then and there the guard tossed Norman up on his shoulders, but he still kept a tight hold on his tail. Norman was sure he was being taken to jail.

You can imagine his surprise when, instead, they entered the museum and heard the artists all clapping and cheering. "Hooray for 'Trapeese'!" they shouted. "Hooray for 'Trapeese'!"

"Well, I'll be bamboozled!" cried the guard. "I do believe you've won a prize! And they're waiting for you to step forward and receive the award!"

The guard rushed up to the judges' platform and said proudly, "Here's the winner! I found him freezing outdoors in the snow!"

"Oh, indeed!" said the head judge, somewhat flustered. "Why, yes—who else could have created the 'daring young mouse on the flying trapeze'? What is your name, my good fellow, and what would you like for your prize?"

"If you please, sir, my name is Norman. I'm the doorman downstairs, and I've always dreamed of seeing the upstairs part of the museum without getting caught. That is what I would like best."

This simple request was granted immediately. Amidst great applause, the guard led Norman out into the Hall, where together they began a grand tour of the entire art museum!

Later that night when Norman returned to his door downstairs he found his mice friends from the country waiting for him there. Of course Norman invited them into his studio, where he shared with them an enormous slice of Cheddar cheese — a present given him by the kindhearted guard. Oh, what a wonderful way to end the day!

Good Knight!